THE SOUL
COLLECTOR

THE SOUL COLLECTOR

BORROWED Souls

BOOK 1

PAUL D KOHLER

Global Endeavor
PUBLISHING

Copyright 2015 by Paul B. Kohler

This title was previously published under the title of Borrowed Souls in March of 2014.

Edited by Amy Maddox
Cover design by Paul B. Kohler
Interior design and layout by Paul B. Kohler

ISBN-13: 978-1-940740-07-2
ISBN-10: 1-940740-07-X

www.paul-kohler.net

Give feedback on the book at:
info@paul-kohler.net
Twitter: @PaulBKohler
Facebook:
facebook.com/Paul.B.Kohler.Author

Printed in the United States of America

First Edition

Chapter 1

Everything was a blur, and I had to force my eyes to focus on the hand touching my shoulder. With effort, the watch on his wrist became clear. It read 1:45. My eyes followed up his arm, to his shoulder, and finally to the person the hand belonged to. The face was covered by several days of growth, and he had crystal-clear eyes.

"Hey, buddy. Last stop," he said, standing above me.

It took me a few moments to realize what was going on. Was this ... heaven? Or was it hell? I tried to stand up but slumped back again.

"Easy now. Had a few too many tonight?" asked the driver.

"Uh, I . . ." is all I could form in my

mouth.

"Don't worry, buddy. I've been there before. You know I'm supposed to call the police when I find a drunk on my bus, but you look harmless enough. Let's get you out to the bench and you can take your time waking up." The driver pulled me up and led me down the aisle of the bus. He helped me down the steps and over to the bench.

Bidding me farewell, the bus driver climbed back in and drove off. I glanced around but nothing looked familiar. To say I was feeling a bit disoriented would be an understatement. As I sat on the cold steel bench, I tried to piece together what might have happened to me. I looked at my watch: 1:53 a.m. Where had the time gone? All I could surmise was that I was extremely late getting home from work and that Cyndi was probably worried.

Despite my throbbing head and the strong desire to curl up on the bus-stop bench to take an extended nap, I forced myself up and began to stagger down the block. As I neared the corner, I looked at the street signs. Neither of the cross streets sounded familiar. I looked in all four directions, wondering which direction home was, and chose the one that looked the most promising.

As I slowly stumbled along the vacant sidewalk, my mind began to retrace my evening. For the life of me, I couldn't even remember even getting on the bus. The last thing I could remember was leaving some café after work. I tried to remember who I was with and kept coming up blank. I must have been with Cyndi. But every time I thought of my wife, I began to feel anger creep into my head. Where was the anger coming from?

After another block of foreign surroundings, I realized I wasn't alone. With my head clearing more by the minute, I slyly glanced back over my shoulder and noticed a man. He was older, dressed in a tan suit with a white fedora. He followed me, keeping pace about a half block behind. Looking forward again I mumbled, "Cyndi, where the hell am I?"

Speaking her name jarred something loose in my head, and the memories from the past twenty-four hours began to resurface. A feeling of loss and despair rushed in, but I could not pinpoint the reason behind it. I felt my pulse rise, anxiety shot to the surface, and my pace quickened. I looked back at the man following me, and he also increased his pace. Not wanting to discover his intentions, I turned the corner, and, once out of sight, I sprinted to the nearest alley.

Ducking into the darkness of the backstreet, I stood in the shadows until the man passed by. He never did. I waited several minutes before I decided to move, and just as I stepped away from the dingy brick wall, a voice came from behind me.

"Feeling a little lost, Mr. Duffy?" The voice was little more than a harsh murmur, but the echo in the alley was thunderous.

I spun around, and the man was standing calmly in the alley. Next to the brightness of his hat, the color of his skin paled in comparison. His eyes were deep and sorrowful as he looked upon me with determination.

"Come again?" I asked.

"It's completely understandable. Riding the M-5 for six hours nonstop would certainly cause bewilderment for anyone," said the mysterious man.

Dumbfounded, I stared at the man. He was a stranger to me, but there was something about him that seemed familiar. "I'm sorry, have we met? You seem to know me by name and know where I was tonight."

"We've not been formally introduced, but rest assured, I'm not here to harm you. What do you remember from last night?" he asked.

"I tell ya', not much. I woke up on the bus, and all I can remember is leaving a café sometime after work. The rest of my day is a blur," I replied, rubbing my temples to soothe an ever-present headache.

"I sometimes find that starting at the beginning of the day is best. Shall we have a seat and begin?" asked the man as he led me across a dimly-lit street to a park bench that I hadn't noticed before stepping into the alley. As unusual as the situation was, it seemed like the right thing to do at the time, so I didn't protest.

"Now then, Mr. Duffy. What was the first thing this morning that you can recall?" asked the man.

"Wait up. Seeing as you know me, maybe you should at least tell me who you are," I stated, hoping to glean as much information about the stranger as I could.

"Come now, Mr. Duffy. You know who I am."

"Sorry, but I really don't. You seem familiar, but I don't remember ever meeting you."

"Oh, that is quite correct. We've not been formally introduced."

"Then what do I call you?"

"Whatever you wish," he said smiling.

"I don't understand. Haven't you got a name?"

"I do, but it doesn't matter what you call me."

We sat on the park bench for several moments in silence; all the while I was racking my brain as to why the last twenty-plus hours were missing from my memory.

"As I mentioned, it might help starting from the moment you woke this morning, or yesterday morning, rather."

The stranger held his closed hand toward me, and when he opened it, there was a large gold coin in his open palm. "Take this coin, Mr. Duffy. Take it and turn it over in your hands. Examine the two faces of the coin, and try to focus on the moment you woke."

I took the coin and did as he asked. The coin was quite old, the surfaces worn nearly smooth. I could just barely make out the words, "In God We Trust," but nothing more. I turned the coin over, and as I did, my morning came flooding back to me.

Chapter 1.5

I rolled over and glanced at the time: 6:43 shone in amber on the nightstand. I reached over and clicked off the alarm. Isn't it strange how one day you can set your alarm and wake up moments before it goes off, but another day you forget and you wake an hour late?

Not wanting to get up, I rolled onto my back, staring at the ceiling. Why did life have to be so demanding? Couldn't I just lie in bed and waste the day away? As I lay in silent contemplation, Cyndi began to stir. I looked over. Her eyes were closed tightly against the rays of morning sunshine beginning to peek through the drapes. I often wished I could be as content with my life as she was with hers. Rarely did anything faze her happy persona.

I reached over and touched the soft skin of her cheek. I could still smell traces of her perfume. The scent was intoxicating. Even after fifteen years of marriage, everything about her made my heart race.

"I love you," I whispered.

"Hrmm?" she mumbled, still in the grasp of sleep.

"I love you, baby," I repeated.

She smiled, eyes still closed. "Me too. You better get up or you'll be late again."

Cyndi was the exemplification of punctuality. I still don't know why she married me. I was late to my own wedding.

"I know. I was just lying here thinking about . . ."

"About what?" she asked, sliding her head over to rest on my chest.

"Work. Life. You. Take your pick," I said as I stroked her hair.

"I'm happy I'm in there somewhere," she replied as she opened her eyes for the first time. Even having just woken, her eyes sparkled brightly.

"What are your plans for today? Want to have lunch?"

She glanced at the clock before answering. Faint frown lines developed between her eyes and she said, "I can't today.

I am volunteering at the Redevelopment Foundation. Remember?"

I did remember but was still hopeful. "Oh right. The foundation. When will you be done?"

"The donation center is open until five, so I should be home around the same as you." She sat up, pushing the covers away. She stretched and tilted her head to the side, her eyes wincing slightly.

"Does it still hurt?" I asked. Cyndi had fallen while rollerblading in the park a few weeks back, and ever since had had neck and backaches.

"Yeah. I was hoping I didn't need to fill the prescription again, but—"

"If it still hurts, fill it. You don't have to take them all."

"Yeah, I suppose. Would you mind picking it up for me today? I'll call it in to the pharmacy near your office."

"Sure thing. Need anything else while I'm there?" I asked, rolling out of bed and reaching for the ceiling in a giant stretch.

"I don't think so. But if something comes to mind, I'll call your office before you leave. Getting off at your regular time?"

"Yeah, probably. Unless Pearlman asks me to stay late for something."

"Just let me know either way," Cyndi said as she lay back onto her pillow, closing her eyes.

Why can't I go back to bed? I asked myself. I shuffled off to shave and shower. Forty minutes later I was dressed and in the kitchen finishing my breakfast. Cyndi sauntered in and sipped from my coffee.

"Don't forget my prescription. I put the slip in your briefcase," she said before vanishing again to shower.

Chapter 2

Feeling beads of sweat slide down my forehead, I used my free hand to wipe them away. I opened my eyes and realized I was still sitting on the park bench next to the stranger. I jumped to my feet, dropping the coin to the ground.

"What the hell just happened? What's going on?" I demanded as I turned to look at the man still sitting casually on the bench. "It was like I was there in my bedroom this morning."

"I assure you, Mr. Duffy, nothing 'is going on'. I'm just here to help you. Think of the coin as a hypnotic device that clears your mind of the unnecessary clutter that slows us all down from time to time." He smiled as he leaned over, picked up the coin, and held it out to me once again.

I sat down and reluctantly took the coin from him. I didn't even have the coin fully turned over in my hand when I was snapped back to my apartment.

Chapter 2.5

After finishing my coffee, I grabbed my briefcase and headed for the elevator. A glance at the clock on the way out told me that I was going to be late. That's all I needed. Punching the elevator call button three times for good measure, I waited a few moments before the familiar ding sounded and the doors parted.

Happiness enveloped me; the eight-foot by eight-foot metal car was empty. Pushing the button for the parking level, the doors closed and the elevator began to drop. My happiness quickly evaporated as the elevator stopped at floor twenty-three. On came Ms. Eastman. "Good morning, Jack," she said, smiling up at me from her four-foot-tall frame.

"Morning, Ms. Eastman." Hoping to avoid an uncomfortable conversation with the building's gossip queen, I pulled Cyndi's prescription from my briefcase and began to read. Thankfully, the elevator doors opened once again a few floors down and on came three more people. Unfortunately, the elevator stopped at nearly every other floor the rest of the way down. After stopping at the lobby to unload most of the passengers, the car dropped two floors farther, letting me and a few others off in the garage.

I climbed behind the wheel of my aging sedan and turned the engine over. After a few cranks, it roared to life. The problem was that the familiar rumble was accompanied by a new knocking sound. I knew it was time for a service, but as the morning was moving along, my mood was drifting swiftly in the wrong direction. The service would have to wait till the weekend.

Unfortunately, I left too late to avoid morning traffic. And although I pulled right into the middle of it, the flow of cars wasn't terrible. I would have been able to make it to work somewhat close to on time if it wasn't for the old woman driving two cars ahead who ran the red light.

The Lincoln Town Car—a yacht on

wheels—plowed into the side of a subcompact heading across her path. Three other cars collided in the intersection as well, bringing traffic to a sudden and unavoidable halt. Yep. I was going to be late for work.

Surprisingly, the emergency vehicles arrived on the scene quickly and were able to restore the morning commute to its natural flow in short order. Short order meaning thirty minutes. Once beyond the bottleneck at the scene of the accident, traffic picked up pace. I was able to pull into my office's parking garage only an hour later than normal.

Chapter 3

I lurched forward uncontrollably, gulping air in an effort to catch my breath. I looked at the stranger, and he only smiled at me knowingly.

"It sounds like the makings for a bad day, Mr. Duffy," he chuckled. "A very bad day. How were your emotions at that point?"

"Honestly, I don't really know. Just now, I started to feel my anxiety increase, but I'm not sure if that's related to the events from earlier or to how I'm experiencing everything again."

"That's understandable and quite expected. Are you ready to continue?"

"Maybe, but—" I paused, thinking of the right way to say what I was thinking. "Why am I doing this? Can't I just call my wife and have her come get me? To tell the truth, it's a little bizarre sitting on a park bench in the early morning, talking to a stranger trying to figure out what happened to my last twenty hours. I still don't know your name," I prompted, hoping to glean more information from the old man.

"Ah yes," he replied, looking at me with a sideways glance. "My given name is Wilson, Wilson Oliver. But I haven't been called that in quite some time. And while you certainly could try to call your wife, where would you have her pick you up from?" asked Wilson as he looked about the vacant park. "Furthermore, what would you tell her about your . . . condition? Honestly, Mr. Duffy, I think it best that we find out what happened to you and your day before going any further with contacting your wife."

Strangely enough, what the old man was telling me sounded logical. I simply nodded and then once again flipped the coin over between my fingers.

Chapter 3.5

After a short ride up the elevator, I was sitting behind my faux mahogany desk ready to dive into my day. There were a few voice messages, each one from my boss, Mr. Pearlman. Listening to each message in succession, Pearlman's voice grew more irate, yet it was still not far from his normal communication level.

After listening to his final message, all I wanted to do was lock my office door and hide until the end of the day. I knew that wasn't going to be an option when Gwen, Pearlman's personal assistant, walked in.

"Good morning, Mr. Duffy. Mr. Pearlman needs to see you right away. Shall I tell him you're on your way up?" she asked, sounding friendly despite working for the asshat of the department.

Even though he was originally in a middle management position below my own, Julio Pearlman was promoted to department chief six months ago. Now he's my freakin' boss. Please, just kill me.

"Uh, yeah. I'll be up in a few minutes. Let me get settled in, it's been a crazy morning."

"Sure thing, Mr. Duffy. I'll tell him you are on your way up," Gwen said, changing my words.

Not being too eager to meet with the man, I took my time sorting my desk to start the day. After several minutes of mindlessly pushing piles of paper from one side of the desk to the other, I took a deep breath and headed for the elevator. As the elevator was mindless of my impending agony, the ride up was mercilessly short and the doors opened directly into Pearlman's lobby. I stepped out and headed toward his office. As I was about to knock, Gwen opened the door and glided out of the office, leaving the door open.

Having known Pearlman since before his promotion, I'd never seen him smile. Not once. Even now he looked particularly unhappy. It was as if he was making a concerted effort to sneer at me. I knew this meeting wasn't going to go well.

"Mr. Duffy, how nice of you to make it in today. You know you're more than an hour late this morning?" Pearlman started off. I stood in silence for a moment, contemplating the best reason to give for my late arrival.

"Well? What do you have to say for yourself? Why were you late? Again, I might add."

"There was—"

"I don't want to hear your excuses!" Pearlman barked. "You're a substandard employee doing a substandard job. If I had my way, you would have been let go a long time ago. And frankly, I'm trying to find a reason why my predecessor even hired you in the first place. This morning's irresponsible action only illustrates my point. Do you think you belong up here with all the other hard-working people of the company?"

Wishing for a rock to either crawl under or crack over Pearlman's head, my tongue was frozen to the roof of my mouth. I couldn't speak to save my life. And honestly, I'm not sure words would have benefited me in any way. Thankfully, Pearlman paused his chastisement long enough to catch his breath.

"I hope you realize, Mr. Duffy, that you are by no means irreplaceable. Your employment here at the company makes no difference to me or to anyone else for that matter. So I believe the choice is yours. You're either here at your desk on time, or you can find another job. Do I make myself clear?"

I decided to stay silent. I knew it would be pointless to argue. Since my morning was deteriorating rapidly, I took the high road. Besides, if I were to point out that the last time I was late was because the parking garage was locked, it would have only prolonged the lecture.

Once Pearlman realized that I wasn't going to give him the rope to hang me with, he barked loudly, "Get out!"

I happily obliged and retreated past Gwen's desk and back down the elevator to my office. I unceremoniously deleted Pearlman's voice messages before digging into my work.

While my PC booted up, I pulled the latest spreadsheet from the mergers and acquisitions project folder and laid it out next to the keyboard. Although an entire team was working on the merger, it was my responsibility to quantify this particular acquisition with hard numbers. Really, it was just busywork, as all the data had been assembled by others. I just needed to find the correct solution to a few key points and send it up the ladder for approval.

The task at hand was to review sales numbers from the target company over the past decade and compare their reaction to world events, religious activities, and technological advancements in the stated period. Even though the work was tedious, I tried my best to stay on task. But I knew that even after spending days on end evaluating the data, it would all end up stuffed in some file folder, never to be seen again. Busywork or not, my professional pride prevented me from treating it as such. The entire report hinged on this one final solution, and despite the speed and accuracy of the modern-day computer, it could not calculate that outcome without the required data.

The morning passed quietly as I stared at various flow charts and spreadsheets. As I switched back and forth between two key charts, I could sense a rhythm in the numbers that I had failed to notice before. As I homed in on a certain string, the answer would dance off the screen, causing me to flip to another document. The drifting of numbers was maddening, but I knew I was close. I stuck with it. I also knew that I couldn't force it, because heading down that rabbit hole was a CLM that I couldn't afford to take.

Pushing the thought of Career Limiting Moves out of my mind, I caught sight of something on the third spreadsheet. Could it be? I quickly shot back to the original document and then back to the modified version. Yes! There it was. The solution was coming into focus. I initiated a few test computations, and although I was certain it would come back green, my pulse rose slightly. As I intently watched the screen for the solution to appear, I was startled by the sound of the phone. Jumping slightly, my hand twitched on the mouse just enough to click the cancel button on the screen.

"God dammit!" I yelled. The computation was gone. The elusive solution was now a whisper in the wind, and I knew I would have to try to retrace the path again.

Chapter 4

"How unfortunate, the timing of that phone call. And you lost all your work up to that point," said Wilson.

"Hmm. It looks like I did," I replied, as I thought about what I had just recited to him. "It's weird. I don't remember any of this stuff happening to me, but as I go through the memories and tell them aloud, I know they are my memories. Why is that? I mean, why are they foreign to me until I tell them out loud?"

Wilson nodded his head as he listened to my question. He sat silent for a few moments before replying. "I am certain the memories are all there inside your head, but there must have been a critical event that caused you to block them from your conscious mind."

"What kind of critical event are we talking about?" I asked.

"Oh, it could be anything from a pet dying to witnessing something disturbing. It quite often varies from person to person, depending on how intense their personal life is. Let's continue," said Wilson as he glanced at his watch.

Chapter 4.5

The phone rang again and again. In my disgust, I snatched up the receiver and barked, "Duffy."

"Mr. Pearlman needs to see you right away," Gwen said on the other end of the line.

"Can it wait until after lunch? I'm at a critical—"

"I'm sorry, Jack, but he said immediately," Gwen said before disconnecting the line.

"I'll be right up!" I said sarcastically to the dial tone in my ear. I began to wonder what he needed me for. I looked at my watch. I had been staring at my computer screen, unmoving, for three straight hours. A distraction might have been welcome, but

Pearlman was not what I had in mind.

As I stepped off the elevator, Gwen nodded in the direction of Pearlman's door as she buzzed me in. This was twice in the same morning that I'd had to stand in front of his unsmiling gaze.

"I need you to run over to that Thai place I like. Get me an order of red curry chicken, an order of pad Thai shrimp, and four spring rolls," Pearlman ordered.

I was again speechless in front of this despicable man. I was about to protest, but he spoke before I could get a word out.

"Listen, Duffy. I know you were probably just wasting your time in your office, and my secretary has more important things to do. Just don't mess this up, and I might consider forgetting about your tardiness this morning. Well? Get moving."

I did the only thing I could do right then without getting fired: I nodded and turned on my heel. As I passed by Gwen's desk, I could have sworn I saw a smirk on her face.

I stopped in my office long enough to jot down Pearlman's order and grab my car keys. Although I could have walked the dozen or so blocks to the Thai place, I felt driving would be quicker. Besides, it was hot out, and I didn't feel like sweating through my last white shirt of the week.

The elevator was quick, and although my car started up relatively easy, my breath quickened when the engine died a moment later. I turned the key again, and after a hint of protest, the engine fired again and away I went.

The lunch hour traffic was expectedly slow, but to my delight, I was able to park right in front of the restaurant. I considered leaving the engine running while I ran into The Catcher in the Thai, but I removed the key out of habit. I double-checked my pocket for the lunch order. Two pats on my breast pocket and I headed into the crowded restaurant.

The air inside reeked of rancid cooking oil laced with a hint of old seafood. The line at the to-go counter was eight souls deep. As it inched forward every five minutes or so, I shuffled my feet and contemplated my project. As much as I hated my job, I constantly dwelled on it. Maybe that was why I hated it so much: because of its silent demand on my attention. Having been passed over for promotion twice in three years, I sometimes wondered if it was worth staying with the company. I was obviously going nowhere, but at least I got a paycheck every other week.

I was so deep in thought, the Hispanic woman behind the counter had to say it again: "Can I take your order?"

I pulled the sheet of paper from my pocket and relayed the order. Her pleasant smile never wavering, she entered the lunch order into the decrepit system and repeated it back to me precisely. I swiped my company credit card and gave the nice woman a twenty-five percent tip. Compliments of Mr. Pearlman, I thought to myself. She handed me a ticket number, and I stepped aside for others to place their order.

As I stood along the wall of the narrow restaurant, I contemplated the irony of a Hispanic woman working at a Thai restaurant in New York. "Only in America," I mumbled. Nobody around me noticed. The patrons were all self-involved with their smart phones.

It wasn't long before they called my order, and as I stepped forward to check that the contents of the Styrofoam containers matched my receipt, the Hispanic woman watched attentively. I nodded at her when I found everything in order. She smiled and nodded her head low.

Once back to the car, I was greeted by an offensive yellow parking ticket tucked haphazardly under the blade of my windshield wiper. By this point in my day, I concluded that the world was in fact out to get me. Thankfully, the car started on the first attempt, and the trip back to the office was unremarkable. Total round-trip for Pinhead Pearlman took just under an hour.

Back up to the sixteenth floor, I stalked right by Gwen and into Pearlman's office. He looked up as I unceremoniously dropped the food on his desk, pulled the receipt stapled to the bag, and read it aloud.

"One order red curry chicken. One order pad Thai shrimp. Four spring rolls." Pearlman looked up from the receipt and scowled profusely in my general direction. "I said curry beef, not chicken." His scowl turned to disgust as he pulled the food containers from the paper bag. "I suppose I can choke it down. Now if you're done bothering me, why don't you get back to work. Isn't your lunch hour just about over?"

The aroma of the food reminded me I had not had lunch myself. I was famished. With my lunch hour wasted on a fool's errand, I hoped I had a snack stashed away in my desk.

"Yes, that sounds about right," I replied. Before leaving Pearlman's office, I pulled the charge receipt from my breast pocket and dropped it on his desk, directly next to the red curry chicken. Smiling, I turned and walked out of his office. Gwen stood poised outside his office, waiting for my exit. As soon as I passed her desk, she slipped in, closing the door behind her.

Chapter 5

"What an incredible douche bag!" I said aloud. "I can't believe he made me his errand boy again."

"This Mr. Pearlman is not a candidate for boss of the year," said Wilson.

"Far from it. He is underqualified and overpaid. He is your run-of-the-mill brownnoser and only got the position because he knows the right people—"

"A baboon could do his job better," Wilson said.

Shocked that Wilson said the exact words I was going to say next, I looked over at the old man. He was still sitting in a casual manner, but the lines between his eyes had deepened, and if I didn't know any better, I would have thought I noticed a bit of compassion in his eyes.

"You are a peculiar man, Wilson. What gives?" I asked.

Wilson whistled softly. "Oh, I've been doing this for more than sixty years."

"And what exactly is it that you've been doing for more than sixty years?"

"I guess you could say I lend an ear to those in need," Wilson said, deftly avoiding the question.

"OK, but how have you been at this for sixty years? You don't look a day over sixty-five. How does that work?"

Wilson fidgeted with the shiny cuff links holding his sleeves tight to his wrists. "That's a whole other matter. One which we have no time to discuss. Please, Mr. Duffy, continue."

Wishing for more information from the old man, but also wanting to get through the rest of the day, I quickly flipped the coin over.

Chapter 5.5

"Pearlman did it again, didn't he?" came a voice from behind me.

Before turning to see who it belonged to, I slid the last of my dollar bills into the vending machine and punched E9, launching the spiral delivery system into motion. The kerplunk echoed throughout the tiny break room, and I pulled out the last candy bar in the machine.

"Hey, Alan. Yeah, Pearlman got me again," I replied before tearing open the plastic wrapper and biting off half the candy bar.

"I'd tell you about lessons learned, but I'm sure you don't want to hear it."

"Here's the thing, Alan: I wrote down the order before I left. He's just a crazy bastard," I replied. "I got him in the end though. I charged it to the company and left the receipt, along with the handwritten food order, on his desk."

"Great! That's one for the peasants. How'd he take it?" Alan asked.

Swallowing the last of my candy bar, I shook my head. "Not sure. I left before he noticed. I thought it best to get out before he realized what had happened."

Alan fell in to stride with me as we walked back to our offices. Alan's office was across the hall from mine.

"Why didn't he just send Gwen?" Alan wondered. "You can't tell me she was too busy typing memos or something."

"No, she was swamped, according to Pearlman. Hell, he even had me get her lunch too."

"Seriously? What did you do to piss that man off? Ever since he got Nelson's job, he's made you his personal bitch. Why don't you stand up for yourself?" Alan asked as we paused outside our office doors.

"I know I should, but I just didn't feel like getting fired today. Besides, he's the department head, and he has his nose buried so far up the VP's ass, he probably knows Snyder's eating habits personally."

"You know he's going to keep doing it until you break."

"Yeah, I think that's what he wants. He's been looking for a reason to get rid of me since day one. You know as well as I do that Pearlman does what Pearlman wants. Isn't that obvious by the string of hot secretaries he's had in the short time he's been here?"

"You really think so?" he asked.

"How many other execs take their secretaries—I mean personal assistants—out to lunch four days a week and then are conveniently busy the rest of the afternoon?" I asked, raising my eyebrows.

"But he's married. I met his wife at the holiday party. They seemed happy together, and she wasn't terrible to look at herself," Alan stated.

"No need to tell me, I was there too," I agreed. "But because you left early, you missed all the action."

"Dammit! How am I just learning about this?" Alan asked.

"I meant to tell you afterward, but it must have slipped my mind."

"Well? What happened?"

"After you left, the two slowly drifted apart, consuming more champagne than should have been possible. Near the end of the night, his wife was flirting with the head of advertising, and Pearlman was trying to fit his head through the neck of his secretary's blouse. It would have fit, too, if it weren't for her still being in it."

Alan whistled quietly. "Seriously, how did none of this make it to the water cooler?"

"Don't you remember that memo that went out after the party?"

"'The dos and don'ts of sex jokes in the workplace'?"

"No, the other one. It came from Snyder himself."

"Ah yes. 'What happens at company parties stays at company parties.'"

"Yep. My guess is Pearlman persuaded Snyder to cover his ass with that one."

"Pathetic."

"I concur. I wholeheartedly concur."

"Tell me, Jack, why didn't you try for the position when Nelson left? You've got a master's degree, and if you ask me, you're the sharpest person on the floor."

"When Nelson was run out of the company, I had no idea the position was open until Pearlman was announced as the new head. Trust me, buddy, I would have given it my best effort if I had been given the opportunity." I shook my head, wondering just how long I would be Pearlman's bitch. Hell, I was even Pearlman's secretary's bitch.

"Listen, Alan, I've got to get back to work. I'm about to crack this code, and I would like to leave here today having accomplished something," I said as I turned in to my office.

"Sure thing. Grab a coffee tomorrow? My treat," Alan offered generously. It was a pity offering, but it felt genuine just the same.

"Always take a freebie. Thanks."

Alan returned to his office as I sat behind my desk.

Flipping on the monitor, I began to review the spreadsheets displayed on the screen. I spent the next fifteen minutes trying to reimmerse myself into my project. However, all I could think about was Pearlman and his bastard ways. As I tried to focus on the equations, my mind reviewed, word by word, the conversation with Alan. What he said made sense. I was the brightest man on the floor. And now that I thought about it, I was the only one around here with a master's degree. I didn't even think Pearlman had one. I began to wonder if that was his motivation to drive me from the company. Feeling my blood begin to boil, I scoured the thoughts from my mind.

I returned to the original document on

my screen, reading the text and scanning the data for the hundredth time. Flipping from document to document, reading and scanning, I felt like my afternoon was going to be a lost cause. I tried my best to recreate my solution, but all I saw was scrambled gibberish. I sat reviewing the lines of data on the spreadsheet that I felt would produce the elusive solution, hands hovering over the keyboard, ready to input the key as soon as it blossomed in my mind.

On my third pass, something deep in my cerebral cortex twitched. I blinked and read the last line again. Could it be? Could I have stumbled across it again? I quickly jotted down the quadrant address on a piece of scratch paper and returned my hands to the keyboard. I blinked fast and felt my heart quicken. I was almost there. I scanned the passage once more, and just as I was about to identify the solution without running any computations, the phone rang.

Snapped back to reality, the solution fluttered away. The phone rang again, and as I contemplated picking it up to tell the caller to go to hell, I calmly pressed the do-not-disturb button on the phone's base and shut down my computer. Had I known how shitty the rest of my day would be, I would have stayed at my desk.

With my office now silent, I grabbed my briefcase and headed for the door. I momentarily popped my head into Alan's office.

"Hey, Alan. I'm heading out—taking the afternoon off as PTO."

"Everything OK?" Alan inquired.

"Yeah, I'm fine. Just need to clear my mind. I'll see you in the morning. If Pinhead comes looking for me, tell him you haven't seen me."

"Will do," Alan said, nodding in compliance.

As I stood waiting for the elevator, I reached into the side pocket of my briefcase to fish out my car keys and found Cyndi's prescription.

"Damn," I mumbled. I had completely forgotten that I promised to pick it up. I glanced at my watch, and as much as I wanted to just get home and forget about the day, it was only a hair past 1:00. I had plenty of time to swing by the pharmacy on the way home.

Minutes later, I was down in the parking garage. I slid the keys into the ignition and turned it over. Nothing happened. I switched it back to off and tried again. Nothing. No dash lights illuminated, no dome light came on. The car was completely dead.

"Shit!" I yelled. I felt like punching the dash. I tilted my head back and began to breathe slowly. It had been months since I last visited my therapist, but I recalled some of the tips he taught me to calm myself in moments of great anxiety. Seeing as my whole fucking day was the poster child for all things stress inducing, I practiced a few.

First, I slowed my breathing to better control my heart rate. Next, I focused on something pleasant: Cyndi, my happy place. I closed my eyes, envisioning her beautiful face in my mind. Finally, I counted backward from twenty, skipping every other number.

"Twenty, eighteen, sixteen, fourteen, twelve, ten, eight, six, four, two, zero," I said aloud, breathing deeply in between each number. Surprisingly, I felt much calmer than the moment before. I no longer wanted to junk punch my car or light a match, toss it in the gas tank, and walk away.

I popped open the glove box, found my roadside assistance number, and dialed it on my cell phone. I explained the situation to the man on the other end of the call, who seemed to think it just needed a jump. He dispatched a driver and said it would be no more than thirty minutes.

Hanging up, I contemplated walking the dozen blocks to the pharmacy but decided against it. As my luck was going, I would get mugged halfway there and miss the tow-truck driver completely. I might even get run over on the way back, I mused. No, no. I waited, sitting on the hood of my car instead. Besides, it was still sweltering out, and walking nearly a mile on the concrete paths of the city didn't remotely appeal to me.

Nearly an hour later, my wait was rewarded by a balding tow-truck driver smelling of stale cigars and burnt motor oil.

"Darn good to meetcha'," he said, pumping my hand a little too aggressively. "What seems to be the problem?"

"Darn thing won't start. I think the battery might be dead, but it just ran a few hours ago," I explained to the overweight man as he popped the hood.

"Well, let's take a look-see," he said as he leaned in near the engine, scrutinizing every part of the grease-covered compartment. "Wanna jump in and give it a try?"

I hopped behind the wheel and turned over the ignition. Nothing happened.

"Go ahead, try and start it," the driver said again.

I turned the ignition back to off and then forward again. Nothing.

"Are you turning the key all the way over?" he asked impatiently.

"I am. I tried it several times just as you asked," I replied, nearing the end of my patience.

"OK, hold on a sec," he said as he jiggled some hoses and wires along the side of the engine compartment. As he did so, I could see sparks fly from under the hood, and the dome light came to life.

"Give it a go," he hollered, still bent over under the hood.

I turned the key to start, and the engine roared to life. "Hurray!" I called out in excitement.

"Looks like you've got a frayed wire leading to the starter. I got 'er fixed for now, but it'll need replacin' soon," said the driver, wiping his hands on a dirty rag hanging out of his side pocket.

"I'll get on that this weekend. What do I owe you?" I asked as I shut the hood.

"Eh, the normal cost for a jump is ninety-five. I really only charge for jumps or tows, but I gotta call this in. Let those that make more than me decide," he said as he climbed into his tow truck.

After several more minutes discussing things on his CB, he popped out with his clipboard in hand.

"Looks like they want me to charge you for the jump anyway. I tried to argue with 'em that it really wasn't a jump, but I lost that battle. You got cash or do you wanna put it on a card?"

"I suppose it makes sense. Here, put it on this," I said, handing him my personal credit card.

"Give me a sec. I'll call it in." He once again disappeared into the cab of his truck only to reappear moments later. "There seems to be a problem with your card here. Got another to try?"

I didn't have the time or the patience for another problem today. "What kind of problem? The card should be paid up and have plenty of room on it."

"Don't know. They jus' said it was declined," he replied, standing close enough that I could smell what could either be rotten eggs or incredibly offensive body odor.

"OK, give this one a try. I know it's good," I said, handing him my corporate card. With the awful day I was having, it was the least Pearlman could do for me. Either that or I'd be fired for abusing company resources.

Five minutes later, the driver returned with a slip for me to sign and a copy of the invoice. I thanked him again, but he wordlessly climbed back into his truck and sped away.

I jumped into the car and blasted the AC before pulling out into the afternoon traffic. I turned up Eighth Avenue and headed toward the pharmacy. Thankfully, traffic was far less hectic than it was that morning or at lunch. I contemplated leaving early every day, just to avoid the traffic. I chuckled at the far-fetched notion, knowing good and well it would never happen.

Ten minutes later I pulled into the parking lot of the pharmacy and found the last parking space available. I left the engine running as I went in to pick up Cyndi's prescription, thinking I would need to call for a jump again otherwise.

Once inside, I fully understood why the lot was full. There was a line at the pharmacist's counter much longer than the line for Pearlman's lunch. I moved to the back of the line and waited. The line moved at a snail's pace, and if I hadn't left work early, I would not have stayed. But as it was only 2:45, I had plenty of time.

Thankfully, another pharmacist opened a

second register and half the people in line moved to equalize the wait. The pregnant woman behind me nearly plowed me over to get into the other lane. I graciously stepped aside. Who am I kidding? I let her over there so she would stop bumping into me with her enormous belly. Seriously, don't people know what personal bubbles are these days?

With the line reduced by half, I progressed to the counter in no time at all. I handed the prescription over and he entered a few things into the computer. A moment later, he handed it back to me and looked at me quizzically.

"Uh, I need to see your ID before I can fill this," he stated.

I slid my driver's license across the counter. The clerk compared it to his screen.

"Hmm. I don't think I can give you this," he said with a confused look.

"Excuse me? You can't give it to me why?" I asked, trying to hold in my rapidly-approaching anger.

"Yeah, the prescription is for oxycodone with acetaminophen. That's a narcotic, and I'm only supposed to give it to the person on the prescription. Your license says you are Jack Duffy, and the prescription's for Cyndi Duffy."

"Ah, I see. Cyndi is my wife. I'm picking it up for her," I replied as calmly as possible. I could feel my anger inching ever closer to the surface.

"Like I said, you're not Cyndi, so I can't give this to you."

"But she's my wife. See, look at my license. We even have the same address. I don't see what the problem is here. I've picked up prescriptions for her in the past."

"The problem? How do I know these pills will even make it to her after I give them to you?" the clerk asked.

"Listen, Clint," I stated, reading his name tag, "I've had very bad day. If you don't find a grown-up back there that can help you out with this, I am going to get pissed. In fact, I might even become irate. NOW FIX THIS!" I yelled, attracting the attention of everyone in line as well as the pharmacist at the other counter.

Clint jumped and took a step back as I barked my orders. He moved to the other pharmacist and the two whispered momentarily. He then disappeared in the stacks of medicines behind them. Moments later, he returned and slid a puffy white envelope across the counter to me along with my driver's license.

"Great. What do I owe you?" I asked, relieved not to be thrown out for making a scene.

"Your insurance covers medication copays," he replied, then he looked at the person behind me. "Next?"

I know I shouldn't have, but I gave Clint the finger as I turned and walked out. It's the little things that help the day move along.

When I stepped back outside, it was getting hotter. I looked at my watch and saw that is was now past three. With any luck, I would make it home by three-thirty, two hours before I normally got home. With that amount of time, I should be able to get in a nap and then maybe cook dinner for Cyndi before she got home.

Chapter 6

After a few minutes of silence, I looked over to the old man. In addition to the frown lines between his eyes, his eyebrows were now furrowed with concern.

"Is there something you're not telling me? You seem to know me, and the recounting of my day hasn't really . . ."

"Has not been a surprise to me," Wilson said, finishing my sentence.

"How are you doing that?" I asked, slightly annoyed that he seemed to be reading my thoughts.

"I am reading your thoughts, Mr. Duffy. It sort of comes with the territory of what I do. I can't read all your thoughts, and not everyone has thoughts that are understandable to me." He quickly straightened his face and smiled. "It's nothing to worry about just yet, Mr. Duffy. I think a bit more recitation and everything will become clear. Please continue."

Without having a better alternative, I flipped the coin.

Chapter 6.5

Fifteen minutes later I pulled into my parking garage. I was happy with myself for making great time despite the heavy traffic. I grabbed my briefcase and jacket and made for the elevator. The ride up was uneventful. I slipped my key into the lock and opened the door.

When I walked in, the first thing I noticed was that the living room lights were on. Cyndi was usually meticulous about conserving energy and almost always walked around the apartment in the dark. Despite my frequent reminders of her own clumsiness, she still did it nightly.

Thinking nothing more of it, I headed to the kitchen for something to drink. That's when I noted the second oddity. Cyndi had left her shoes lying in the middle of the floor, and I spotted a few used plates left on the kitchen counter. My lovely wife must have come home early. Her back pain must have been more severe than she had let on that morning.

Not wanting to wake her, I tiptoed down the hall and slowly opened the bedroom door. Within seconds I heard the noises.

Curious, I pushed the door fully ajar. The shades were drawn; the room dark. Despite the dimness, I could see Cyndi in bed, but she certainly wasn't sleeping. In the shadowy glare from the hallway behind me, I could make out an additional body. I stepped to the side, allowing more of the light to spill across the bed. I could see the shape of not one but two people entwined, covered by the thin bed sheet. The actions I witnessed fully aligned with the sounds emanating from the bed. They were fucking.

My knees began to weaken beneath me. Frozen and unable to move, all I could do was watch in horror. There I was, standing in the doorway of my bedroom, watching my wife having sex with another man. My chest began to tighten. My breathing quickened. I was horrified, but I couldn't move.

I finally forced my legs to move. I slowly

backed out into the hallway, pulling the door to its original position. I retraced my steps through the apartment and back out into the corridor. I left the front door open, not caring whether Cyndi knew I had been home or not.

Chapter 7

I had no words to describe what I was feeling. The old man cleared his throat, but I paid him no attention. All I could think about was what I had just witnessed—for the second time. Sadness turned to anger. I could feel my soul moving inside me, and I had to do something or else I felt like I would explode. I stood and walked to the edge of the dirt path near the park. From where I stood, I could see the sky grow a shade lighter. Dawn was approaching, and here I was, standing in an unknown park, speaking to a strange man about the most fucked up day I've ever had. Cyndi and I used to love sunrises. How ironic, I thought.

"Did you know?" I asked the old man, who was now sitting straight up. It was as if he had prepared himself for an onslaught of questions.

"I cannot say what I knew exactly. The answer to you would prove confusing at best," he replied, making zero sense to me.

"Was that the event that caused my memory block?" I asked, taking a seat next to him.

"That might have something to do with it, but according to my calculations," he paused to look at his watch again, "you are still missing an hour or so before getting on that fateful bus ride."

I nodded. I had assumed as much. Coin in hand, I continued my trip down memory lane.

Chapter 7.5

Delirious, I made my way back to the elevator and gently pressed the call button. I stood there, waiting, my mind in a fog. As the elevator dinged, there was a cry coming from the direction of my apartment. It was Cyndi, now dressed in a robe, standing just outside our apartment door. The doors parted, and I casually stepped in to the elevator. I pressed the button for the lobby, and as I turned around I could hear running footsteps. Cyndi came into view at the precise moment the elevator doors closed her face off from me - forever.

The elevator made its descent to the first floor in less than a minute. I walked out into the penetrating heat and turned right down the sidewalk. I was numb, and had no particular destination in mind. I just needed to walk away.

The sidewalks were beginning to fill with the daily workforce leaving for the evening. The farther I walked, the more crowded the sidewalks became. Having no real plan, I decided I would step off the concrete path of civilization and have a seat.

A block later, I came upon a little bistro with a small outdoor courtyard. I moved through the entry and out onto the terrace. I sat along the outside railing, and a waiter brought me a menu and a glass of water.

Despite the cover on the patio, the heat was nearly unbearable. Moving to a table inside never crossed my mind. I just sat in the silence, wondering why this day was destined to be so disastrous. There was nothing left for fate to deface.

I sipped from the glass of water, feeling its cool tingle as it passed my lips. I looked around the patio and realized I was alone. My soul was just as alone. I wondered what I should be feeling. Hate? Fear? Anger? I felt them all but none at the same time. I felt like crying but couldn't find the energy. I thought about calling my therapist but dismissed the thought. I knew what he would tell me: it was all going to be OK. How on earth was it going to be OK? My wife, the center of my world, had just cheated on me. My job was horrendous. My entire life seemed to be in a tailspin heading for a fiery crash.

I suddenly realized that throughout the last thirty minutes, I had been carrying my briefcase. Why hadn't I set it down in the apartment when I walked in? I sat it on the ground next to my chair and saw Cyndi's prescription. I pulled it from the side pocket and laid it on the table in front of me. I took another sip of water and began to read the label.

I scanned through the generic warnings and precautions. Toward the end of the label, it mentioned that the side effects could be numbness and drowsiness. That sounded about right. I tore open the sealed envelope and popped the lid off the bottle. I emptied a handful of pills onto the table in front of me and contemplated my future.

What exactly did my future hold? I no longer had a wife that loved me. Hell, did she ever love me? I had a boss that would be happy to see me thrown out onto the street. I had no kids, thankfully. Both my parents had passed away years ago. I had nothing left at all. I knew right then that nobody would ever miss me. I took another drink.

Having dealt with depression for many years, I was no stranger to the thought of suicide. Hell, I think everyone thinks about the what-ifs of suicide at least once in their life. I just happened to have thought about it many times over the years. Through countless sessions with my therapist, we concluded that the depression stemmed from mass bullying throughout primary school. The feeling of hatred was still strong toward the people that caused me so much pain. At that moment, random neurons in my brain connected two events in my live, separated by nearly 20 years. Pearlman was the coalescence of all the bullies of my youth.

And there I sat, contemplating my future, my mortality. Whether or not to take my own life. I looked from pill to pill. I knew how easy it would be to end all the pain and suffering. Just a handful of pills and a quick gulp of clean, cool water would be so easy.

I reached up and wiped a bead of sweat from my brow and glanced around once more. I tried to think of a single reason not to take the pills, but nothing came to mind. All that I could think about was seeing my wife move rhythmically with another man.

Chapter 8

"Please, God, no!" I said, barely containing my growing anxiety. "Please tell me," I begged.

"You were supposed to wait for me on the bus," he said.

"Why's that?" I said turning fully in Wilson's direction.

The old man held his hand out, producing an amber-colored prescription bottle out of thin air. He gave the bottle a shake, rattling the remaining Percocet pills inside.

"Who are you?" I asked, afraid I already knew the answer to the question.

"You already know who I am," he replied.

"All right then. Why are you here?"

"I think you know the answer to that

question as well."

I nodded my head in agreement. Although yesterday was an absolutely horrific day, now I wasn't entirely sure I wanted to die. A terrible job and a cheating wife were no reasons to end a life, and all it took was a kind stranger and a bus ride to figure that out.

"Did I really take all those pills?" I asked, looking down at the coin still in my hand.

"Why not find out for yourself? You've come this far, but I wouldn't think less of you for not wanting to see your final moments."

Before I had a chance to decide, my subconscious mind made the choice for me. I turned the coin for the final time."

Chapter 8.5

As a tear rolled down my cheek, I reached for a pill and placed it on my tongue. I instinctively swallowed it without water. A moment later, I took two more. I sat there waiting for something to keep me from taking the whole pile, but nothing did. I scooped the remaining pills from the table and tossed them back all at once. I washed them down with the last of my water.

Not wanting to cause a scene at the quaint little restaurant, I slid the pill bottle into my pocket and left the patio through the side exit. Back on the sidewalk, I meandered aimlessly for few blocks before coming to a bus stop. With no motivation to proceed, I sat on the bench.

Leaning back, I wondered how long the

pills would take and how it would happen. Having never used pain medications, I was unsure what the effects would be. All I felt was anxiety.

As the moments passed, I thought about what I had witnessed. Seeing Cyndi with another man was an absolute betrayal that I would have never imagined. Not for the first time, I asked myself how she could do it. Had our love for each other meant nothing to her?

I tried to figure out where our relationship might have gone wrong, but thinking back to our last fight some six months previous, nothing stood out. That last fight was over something stupid, like leaving dishes unrinsed in the sink. It wasn't really the dishes that the fight was about, but it certainly was the igniter. The fight carried on for several days, and every little idiosyncrasy fueled the argument. Finally, after I was tired of being mad at her for being mad at me, I apologized, and all was better. So I thought. Could that have been the reason? Could that have made her look at me differently? Surely not, I mused.

I felt so alone.

Moments later, I noticed my breathing begin to change. It felt as if I could not get enough air in my lungs. I tried to take in larger breaths, but just as soon as I inhaled, I involuntarily let the breath out. My accelerated breathing caused my heart to beat faster. I didn't notice it right away, but once my hand began to twitch, I knew it was from the pills. I leaned my head back and tried to relax, but the combination of the traffic noise and the overdose of pills prevented me from doing so.

Then, out of nowhere, it felt like my stomach flipped a somersault. I quickly leaned forward, and as I did, I knew I was going to puke. I looked up and down the street for a garbage can, but none were in sight. With no other alternative, I stood up and staggered to the curb. Leaning over, I threw up what little food I had eaten through the day. I spat out the languishing bile in my mouth and tried to stand up. A sudden dizzy spell took over, and I nearly collapsed backward. I reached out and grabbed the signpost to steady myself. I felt the time was near. I figured it would be quick, but I had no idea that the pills would affect me so soon.

As I stood there, a man walking by stopped next to me and asked "You doing OK, man?"

Although confusion was setting in, I heard the man's words and nodded. When I looked into the man's eyes, I saw worry and concern.

He patted me on the shoulder and continued down the sidewalk. For a brief moment, I wondered if I had made the wrong choice by taking the pills.

A moment later, a city bus pulled to a stop right in front of me. It took me a moment to realize that I was still standing at the bus stop. I instinctively pulled my bus pass from my wallet and climbed aboard. In typical fashion, the first several rows of the bus were filled, so I moved to the very last row and slumped down. The bus lurched ahead, and I felt as if I had left my stomach back at the stop. I leaned forward, feeling like I was going to puke again, but it was just dry heaves. There was nothing left in my stomach.

I looked around at the other passengers on the bus. They were all on their time schedule. Most were just getting off work and heading home, while others were heading in the other direction. For me, time had no meaning. Unlike those around me, I had no pressing matters. I knew the end was near. The pungent odors of sweat and unwashed bodies drifted about the cramped vehicle, but I was unfazed. Nothing bothered me. I leaned back and smiled. For the first time all day, I felt contentment.

As moments passed for me, hours passed for the others in the world. I drifted in and out of consciousness, waiting for the end to take me. It wasn't until the jostle that my eyes opened.

Chapter 9

"So, am I dead then? Is that why you're here?"

"Well, yes and no. I'll explain." He pulled a white handkerchief from his breast pocket and dabbed it across his forehead. "You see, much like yourself, I was late today. Actually, I need to correct that. I was with you earlier, but it wasn't at the proper time, so I left you to take care of another matter. When I returned to you, you had in fact died but had miraculously come back to life."

"If I'm alive, then why are you still here? I can go now, right? I got a second chance?" I eagerly suggested.

"It's not like that, Mr. Duffy." He paused and slid the refolded handkerchief back into his outer pocket. "You did die. And as soon as you took those pills, you set a number of other events in motion. So, per my orders, I need to take your soul. You see, I'm a soul collector."

"But you said I miraculously came back to life. Doesn't that mean I am, in fact, a miracle myself?"

"In all the years of doing this job, Mr. Duffy, I have only witnessed a similar event one other time."

"And what happened then?" I asked.

Wilson looked down to the ground. "What happened then doesn't matter now. What does matter is I need to turn in a soul, and yours is the one that needs collecting."

We sat in silence, both of us staring at anything but each other. I thought about getting up and running. At his age, it would be no contest.

"Yes, you could run, Mr. Duffy, but it would be pointless," Wilson stated matter-of-factly.

"How'd you . . . never mind."

"I know more than you could ever imagine, Mr. Duffy. I know things sometimes before they occur."

"If that's the case, how'd you miss me dying? Wouldn't you have foreseen that as well?"

"Excellent point. With my advanced age, it appears that I might be losing my edge. You see, time passes slower for me than it does for the living. Much slower. For every one of my hours, eight of yours passes. That's why I thought that I would have been able to collect another soul and still have time to get back to you. The other soul had fallen from a building at a construction site near here. Poor fellow. He left a loving wife and three children behind."

"Oh," is all I could think of to say in response. I thought this process would be different.

"Different in which way?" asked Wilson.

"Well, I guess I never thought someone like you would age at all. Granted, I never really thought about what happens after death in the first place. Earlier you said it was too late for second chances and something about other events set in motion. Any chance we could stop them?"

"Here's how it works. Society has a specific number of souls in use, with new souls being generated as demand sees fit. Those new souls are developed at an established rate that was predetermined a millennia ago. Once a person dies, their soul is recycled into a new birth. You've heard the term 'old-soul'? Well, that just means the soul has been through many lives. There are far more old souls than there are new souls in the world."

"I find all this extremely interesting, Wilson, but how does me coming back to life affect any of this?"

"Every time a person dies, a new birth is in line to accept their soul. Your soul has been claimed, and the birth is imminent. As all the new souls have been claimed to date, your soul needs to be moved along within a reasonable time frame."

"And my soul is the only one available? People die all the time. You can't tell me that there aren't other souls that can be put into place."

"I understand your apprehension, Mr. Duffy, but those other souls are being placed into their assigned births all the time. Tomorrow's quota might be—will be—completely different than it was for today." Wilson paused a moment. "Listen, Mr. Duffy. I need a soul to turn in, and I cannot understand your sudden resistance. After all, you did in fact attempt to end your life. Even if I could let you live, your life would never be the same. The fact that your wife committed adultery would not change. Can you honestly tell me you would happily take her back just to avoid moving on to the afterlife?"

"I guess I really didn't think about that. Isn't there a way to go back a few days earlier?"

"I'm not a miracle worker. I'm not a time traveler. I'm here only to collect your soul."

Hearing the finality of Wilson's words, I had never felt more alone. I began to cry.

After several moments of silence, Wilson spoke. "Suppose I had an alternative—"

"Name it," I replied quickly, wiping the tears from my cheeks. "I'll take whatever you've got to offer."

"Slow down, Mr. Duffy. You might not like what I have to offer. It most certainly will not give you the life you've become accustomed to."

"I'm listening."

"You see, I have been doing this for sixty-one years now, and when I became a soul collector, I was fifty-seven."

"Wait, what? How is that possible?"

"I died when I was fifty-seven. I had a heart attack and was brought back to life. I was dead for several minutes, and because there happened to be no more new souls available at the time, a used soul needed to be collected. The soul collector at the time of my death had been doing her job for quite some time. I also didn't want to cease to exist, so we turned in her soul instead. In other words, she retired."

"OK, I think I get that, but the math doesn't make sense."

"It's the eight-to-one ratio that is probably throwing you off. Think of it like this: I continued to age at the same rate as everyone else, but I lived eight times longer. If I hadn't become a soul collector, I would be sixty-six, although I would have been that age more than fifty years ago."

I started to comprehend the difference in time as Wilson explained it. That's when it hit me.

"So, just like that? You're ready to retire?" I asked.

"It's not as spontaneous as it appears, Mr. Duffy. Like I said, I've been at this for sixty-one years. I'm getting tired. I've been contemplating moving on for many years, and I think I'm finally ready." He looked at me as if sizing me up. "You see, I've been on the lookout for someone to take over for me. That person is you."

"What happens next for me?"

Wilson held both of his hands out, palms up. As I looked at them, a small wooden box appeared on each hand. A name was carved on the lid of each box. One box had my name, Jack Duffy. On the other box, Wilson Oliver was carved. The box with Wilson's name was much older than my box.

"If you take over being a soul collector, you will take both of these boxes. The box with your name will be yours to keep until you feel it's time to retire. At your current age of thirty-five, you would almost certainly be able to live into the twenty-fourth century."

"Done! Let's do this," I replied excitedly.

"Not so fast, Mr. Duffy. There are consequences. You would not be able to talk to anyone from your previous life again. The only conversations permitted would be with the dead or dying, much like I am speaking to you now. Trust me when I tell you that it gets quite lonely."

"Wilson, I've lived the last five years of my life in relative solitude. Besides my wife, who just cheated on me, I had no real friends. I don't see a big difference."

Wilson nodded in agreement. "I knew that was going to be your response. Once you take these boxes from me, you cannot go back. You will be a soul collector from now until you turn in your soul. This is just prolonging the inevitable."

"I get it. I'm in till I retire. I can do this," I replied.

"OK then, Mr. Duffy. Take the two boxes from my hands. Once you possess them, open the box with my name on it and hold it open toward me."

"Wait. What happens to you?"

"I'm retiring, boy. Haven't you been paying attention?"

"Yes, I get that. But will you just cease to exist? What about your body?"

"I will become an unknown death in the current year, and you will capture my soul in this box. You will then turn in that soul and get another empty box. You will continue to fill boxes with collected souls until you retire."

"OK, but how do I collect souls? Will there be some sort of training?"

Wilson laughed out loud. "You ask too many questions. Once you take the boxes, all will become clear."

I took a deep breath as I reached for the boxes in Wilson's hands. Just before I slid them from his hands, I paused. Our eyes met, and I could have sworn I saw a twinkle in his. I held my hands next to his, palms up. Wilson rotated his hands on to mine, transferring the boxes to me simultaneously.

He lifted his hands in the air, and now it was his turn to lean back to relax. I turned the boxes over in my hands, examining each of them individually. I thought about sliding my box into my pocket, but before I could, it vanished. Startled, I looked up at Wilson.

"Things will be much different for you from now on, Mr. Duffy. You will have, shall we call it, practical magic at your disposal from this point forward."

"Cool."

"Now if you would, open my box and hold it out in front of me."

"What? That's it? You pawn off the boxes on me and you're out of here?" I asked, astounded. I wondered if I had just made yet another bad choice.

"There's nothing left to say. I've lived my life—both in reality and in the afterlife. What would you have me say or do that would make a difference?"

"Well, for purely selfish reasons, can you give me any tips? Do I eat, and if so how often? How about sleep? And when does happy hour start?"

Wilson laughed. "Sorry, there's no happy hour, Mr. Duffy. The only tip I will give you will be the same advice that my predecessor gave me." He paused as he placed his hat atop his head. He sat straight up, looking at me eye to eye.

"Forgiveness is a virtue that needs to be nourished. Resentment only leads to disappointment."

"That's it? That's your sage advice? I was hoping—"

Wilson continued, "And listen to Hauser. He is wise well beyond his years."

I nodded silently, not because I had no words, but because I couldn't breathe. I wasn't choking or gasping for breath, but there was no air in my lungs to speak.

"Now, if you please. Open the box and I'll be on my way," Wilson said with his own last breath.

I did as Wilson requested. I opened the box and looked inside before turning it toward him. The inside of the box was just as plain as the outside but without any signs of wear. I turned the box around and held it open toward Wilson. "What now?" I asked, suddenly able to speak.

Wilson closed his eyes and began to sing a song. The words sounded familiar, but I couldn't place it. As he sang, I began to notice a wisp of smoke or fog leaving his mouth. It lifted out and away from his lips. Once the trail of smoke was completely out of him, his voice ceased, and the paleness of his skin dulled as he slumped back against the bench. The cloud began to move through the air in the direction of the wooden box. Once it completely entered the box, the lid closed on its own and instantly vanished. In its place, another box appeared. The new box looked just like my box, but the name was different.

The name on the box was Cyndi Duffy.

ABOUT THE AUTHOR

When not practicing architecture, Paul works on his writing. He lives in Littleton, Colorado, with his wife and daughter.

To learn more about him and his books, visit www.Paul-Kohler.net

Made in the USA
Middletown, DE
30 September 2017